For Phoebe Anabel Jones – A.G.

For Molly, always my inspiration – S. McN.

ORCHARD BOOKS

First published in Great Britain in 2003 by Orchard Books

This edition published in 2004 by The Watts Publishing Group

17

Text © Adèle Geras, 2003

Illustrations © Shelagh McNicholas, 2003

The moral rights of the author and illustrator have been asserted.

A CIP catalogue record for this book is available from the British Library.

ISBN 978 1 84362 413 4

Printed and bound in China

Orchard Books

An imprint of

Hachette Children's Group

Part of The Watts Publishing Group Limited

Carmelite House

50 Victoria Embankment

London EC4Y 0DZ

An Hachette UK Company

www.hachette.co.uk

www.hachettechildrens.co.uk

# The Ballet Class

Written by
Adèle Geras

Illustrated by
Shelagh McNicholas

ORCHARD

It's Tuesday. It's ballet class day!
My favourite day of the week.
Mum calls me Tutu Tilly because
I love ballet so much.

At the dance studio, we all put on
our special ballet clothes.
I've got a pretty pink leotard
and tutu to wear.

Katie's leotard
is lilac.

Ballet clothes aren't very easy to get into.

Miss Anne, our teacher, claps her hands to start the class. This is the last lesson before our big show, so we must all practise extra hard.

We do warm-up exercises first.
Katie likes

'happy back,

grumpy back'

because she's good
at that, but I like

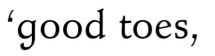

'good toes,

naughty toes'.

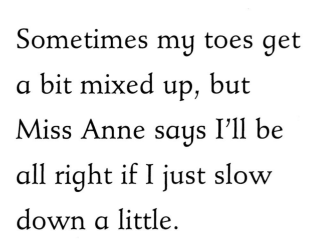

Sometimes my toes get
a bit mixed up, but
Miss Anne says I'll be
all right if I just slow
down a little.

Next we go through our positions:

first,

second,

third,

fourth,

and fifth.

Then we practise our
**curtsies**
to the queen,

and **bows**

to the king.

Mrs Howard plays a butterfly tune on the piano and we **flutter** and **float** and **flap** our butterfly wings.

Then the music changes.
**Thump! Crash! Whump!**
It's a dinosaur song! We all
stamp and clomp in time to it.
Jake loves being a dinosaur!

We do leg bends and jumps next. Miss Anne calls them **pliés** and **jetés**.

That's leg bends and jumps in French.

When our mums and dads come
to collect us, Miss Anne says:
"Remember to practise your own dances
for the show next week, please."

I practise my show dance every single day.
I want to be just like a real cat:

a leapy cat,

a curled-up-to-sleepy cat,

a stretchy cat,

a pounce-on-a-mousey cat.

I can't wait for the show on Tuesday.

On the day of the show,
everyone's excited.
We all change into our
special costumes. I have a long,
velvety tail and ears, and Mum draws
whiskers on my cheeks with face paints.

My tummy feels funny.
Mum says it's full of
butterflies because
I'm a bit nervous.

The music starts and we all run on to the stage. I swish my tail. First, I'm a tiptoe-on-my-paws cat, then I'm a fierce show-all-my-claws cat.

I'm the most perfect cat I can be.
Jake is a growly bear and Katie
swoops round the stage
like a bluebird.

When the show is over, everyone claps very loudly and we do our best curtsies and bows. I wave at my mum and dad.

Miss Anne tells us we all danced beautifully. Mum says my dance was lovely. Dad says he thought I was a real cat.

I say, "Miaow!" which means thank you!

Now I can't wait for next Tuesday. I LOVE ballet!